DR XARGLE'S BOOK OF EARTH WEATHER

A Red Fox Book. Published by Random House Children's Books,
20 Vauxhall Bridge Road, London SW1V 2SA.

First published in 1992 by Andersen Press Ltd. Red Fox edition
1994. Text © Jeanne Willis 1992. Illustrations © Tony Ross
1992. All rights reserved.
Printed in Hong Kong

3 5 7 9 10 8 6 4

RANDOM HOUSE UK Limited Reg. No. 954009
ISBN 0 09 929941 0

DR XARGLE'S BOOK OF EARTH WEATHER

Translated into Human by Jeanne Willis
Pictures by Tony Ross

Red Fox

Good morning, class.

Today we are going to learn about the weather on planet Earth.

There are four sorts.
Too hot. Too cold. Too wet and too windy.

Unlike us, earthlets are not waterproof. They go soggy in the rainblob. They must put on a loose, plastic skin.

Some grow large rubber feet. These are impossible to remove.

To stop water getting into their one small brain they carry material on a pointed stick with sharp prongs. This is a dangerous weapon. Sometimes it attacks its owner.

When many brollies get together they always go for the eyes.

Mad earthounds and earthlings go out in the mid-day sun. The earthlings strip to their underfrillies and rub each other with fat.

Then they lie on the floor in the shape of a star.
When they go brown it means they are cooked.

Never eat them.

Sometimes an earthling cooks for too long. The only cure is to creep up and slap him on the back.

To avoid this, sensible earthlings put a nostril wiper on their heads, roll up their legs and stand in the briny ocean.

Earthlings suffer badly with the wind. Here are some things to avoid on breezy days.

Wearing a pretend hairdo.

Wearing a big frock in public.

Eating pink knitted sugar on a stick.

In winter, the planet is invaded by strange white
earthlings with black eyes and orange noses.

They hold brooms but refuse to do the sweeping. They stand still all day smoking their pipes.

Small earthlets find it hard to stand up and must be dragged around on a block of wood.

Warlike earthlets fling missiles of ice at the enemy.

To protect themselves they wear handcosies and a puffed garment called anorak. It must be knotted tightly around the gargle with two toggles.

Failure to do so may result in the helmet being
secretly stuffed with ice missiles by another earthlet.

That is the end of today's lesson. Put on your disguises and gather your carol sheets.

We are going to perform on the doorstep of the earthlings. Matron tells me it is the custom to do this in their month of July.

All together now, "Hark the horrid angels sing...."

Some bestselling Red Fox picture books

THE BIG ALFIE AND ANNIE ROSE STORYBOOK
by Shirley Hughes
OLD BEAR
by Jane Hissey
OI! GET OFF OUR TRAIN
by John Burningham
DON'T DO THAT!
by Tony Ross
NOT NOW, BERNARD
by David McKee
ALL JOIN IN
by Quentin Blake
THE MOON'S REVENGE
by Joan Aiken and Alan Lee
BAD BORIS GOES TO SCHOOL
by Susie Jenkin-Pearce
WE CAN SAY NO!
by David Pithers and Sarah Greene
MATILDA
by Hilaire Belloc and Posy Simmonds
WILLY AND HUGH
by Anthony Browne
THE WINTER HEDGEHOG
by Ann and Reg Cartwright
A DARK, DARK TALE
by Ruth Brown
HARRY, THE DIRTY DOG
by Gene Zion and Margaret Bloy Graham
DR XARGLE'S BOOK OF EARTHLETS
by Jeanne Willis and Tony Ross
JAKE
by Deborah King